3/11

For all boorai
    Trees, rivers, seas
for Mum + Dad, my family, amazing friends

and everybody who loves a laugh

ALLEN&UNWIN

PEKA-BOO

THE SMALLEST BIRD IN ALL THE   WORLD.

Eliza Feely

Life as The Smallest Bird in All the World can be tough-witchetty.

First I had to crack an egg 20 times my size.

It took months to see sun.

My arrival was a real gobdropper.

I learnt quick-sticks to grab attention like a bull ant.
It's no skip in the bush you know.

Getting lost is easier than chucking rocks in a puddle.

Sometimes I get lost to have a rest from staying found.
Sure as apples drop my muggins brothers will muddle my peace.

They love to tease me.   It's funny.

But not when you can't keep up.

Nothing fits.

Mum tells me that
   being the Smallest Bird in All the World is tremendous.

She reckons the mere sight of me puts real pep in her hop.

But her eyesight's on the blink.

Being seen is a breeze.   A bore.

Or

spectacularly tricky.

It depends on my mood.

If I overdo tricky   Mum says,   Right. That's it feral feathers.
It's time you learnt a thing or two about a thing or two.

And I have to stay with Kapecki,

the oldest,   weirdest   near-deaf bird in the bush.

I HATE BEING THE SMALLEST BIRD IN ALL THE WORLD!

Pardon?   Says Kapecki.

And what's SOOOOoooo funny?

Because Kapecki laughs all the time.

What's so funny? I ask.

And he just

NwWaaaHaHaHa
oOOoKKKaHaHaHa
HaHaakakahHaHa
HaHaMaaHaWhooHoo
HaMaHaHaHa
HaHaHaHa
Ha

Seriously. What a weirdo.

The thing is Kapecki doesn't care how small I am.

With him, being the Smallest Bird in All the World doesn't matter a pip.

Who cares
if he's older than Uluru
and as deaf as a log.

Not me!
He's the King!

Don't give a twig.
Nup, not a bit.

And I didn't.

Until the day Kapecki got so old he couldn't see me anymore.

But Kapecki thought I'd gone for good.

He was so sad he stopped laughing   and   turned stone quiet.

It was awfully odd.

I started to cry.

In the silence I heard Kapecki in my mind.

You can't make worm pie . . . from . . . a . . . stack of bracken.

I thought about it.

(It made me hungry.)

Mid rumble something inside me tweaked.

Warrrble deedooo
llaeelelelelePip
Pipa aa warrpip
eeaa aa aaqapip
waaee aa
a

I foofed my feathers, and warbled a doozey 'til my lungs went flat.

Waaaarble
dooWarble
aaarr
eeee
eel
el
e
e
e
e

I tried again, only a little higher.

Out of the blue popped a HUGE   orange note!

What the Bunyip! Honked Kapecki.

PEKA-Booooo??? Is that . . .

Hooley Dooley. Said Kapecki, stunned.

You had me worried you little flibjippiter, he cackled.

Everything was topsy turvy. But I felt giddy with relief. I was as . . .

free   as   a   breeze.

with seed-cracking gusto.

I could warble to the WHOLE WORLD if I wanted.

So I did.

I do every day.

First
published in 2008

Allen & Unwin
83 Alexander St
Crows Nest NSW 2065 Australia
Phone: (61 2) 8425 0100
Fax: (61 2) 9906 2218
Email: info@allenandunwin.com
Web: www.allenandunwin.com

National Library of Australia
Cataloguing-in-Publication entry:

Feely, Eliza.
Peka-boo, the smallest bird in all the world

ISBN: 978 1 74175 541 1 (hbk.)

A823.4

Design by Eliza Feely and Bruno Herfst
Set in 18 pt Traveling Typewriter
Printed in China through Colorcraft Ltd, Hong Kong

With a huge thank you to Jodie, Erica, Bruno, Chloe & the Caralieros, Nick P, Greg,
Lindy, Athena, BTG, Sim, Chris, Jason, Meryl, David, Am, Geoff, Mum, Dad, Simone B and Damian
who were instrumental in the making of this book.

This book is printed on 100% recycled paper

10 9 8 7 6 5 4 3 2 1

www.allenandunwin.com